Just Like Dad

Based on the TV series *Little Bill*® created by Bill Cosby as seen on Nick Jr.®

 SIMON SPOTLIGHT

An imprint of Simon & Schuster Children's Publishing Division
1230 Avenue of the Americas, New York, New York 10020

Manufactured in the United States of America
First Edition   10 9 8 7 6 5 4 3 2 1
ISBN 0-689-83999-5

JUST Like Dad

by Kim Watson
based on the original teleplay "The Bills Go to Work" by James Still
illustrated by Daniel M. Kanemoto

Simon Spotlight/Nick Jr.

New York   London   Toronto   Sydney   Singapore

Little Bill was having a great time riding on his father's back.

"Giddyap, horsey! Faster, faster!" he called out.

"This old horse is too tired to go any faster," Big Bill replied, but he galloped around the room again.

"Okay, time for all cowboys to mosey on off to bed," said Little Bill's mom, Brenda, as she walked in.

"Dad, can we play horsey in the morning, before I go to school?" Little Bill asked.

Big Bill smiled. "You've got the day off from school tomorrow, partner. I guess you forgot."

"I do? The whole day?" Little Bill asked.

"That's right, a whole day off. And I've got special plans for us," Big Bill said as he galloped up the stairs.

"What, Dad, what?" Little Bill asked.

"You're going to work with me," Big Bill answered.

"I am? Yahoo! I'm going to work— just like you!" shouted Little Bill.

"What's going to work like, Dad?" Little Bill asked.

Big Bill thought hard. "Let's see. Going to work is kind of like going to school."

Big Bill explained that sometimes he had to sit quietly and listen. Other times he talked and laughed with his friends. Just like Little Bill.

"Do you like work, Dad?" Little Bill asked.

Big Bill laughed. "Yep, I sure do," he said.

"Then I'm going to like it too," Little Bill said. "I can't wait to go to work with you."

Big Bill smiled and kissed Little Bill. "Good night, son."

Little Bill sat in bed and looked out the window. He began to imagine.

Little Bill imagined he was in school with his dad. They played and laughed. They sang songs and built skyscrapers out of wooden blocks.

Little Bill showed Big Bill how to finger paint, and they painted pictures of rocket ships and dinosaurs.

And when it was time for dancing, Little Bill taught his dad all the right moves.

He loved having his dad for a playmate. If work was anything like this, it was going to be fun!

When Little Bill woke up the next morning, he yawned and stretched. He thought about what he was going to do at school that day.

Then he remembered something. "I'm going to work with Dad today! Woohoo!" he cried.

"Do you always shave before you go to work, Dad?" asked Little Bill.
"Yep," answered Big Bill. And he spread shaving cream all over Little Bill's face.
Little Bill looked in the mirror and giggled. "Me too!"

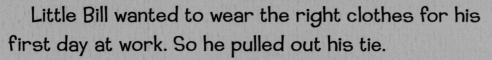

Little Bill wanted to wear the right clothes for his first day at work. So he pulled out his tie.

"Well, look at that," Big Bill said when he saw Little Bill. "You've got a tie just like mine."

"Yep, I'm going to be just like you," Little Bill said proudly.

At breakfast April looked across the table at her dad and Little Bill. "You look like twins," she said, chuckling.

Little Bill looked at his father. "Look, Mama, we're twins," Little Bill said.

"Very *handsome* twins," Brenda said.

Just then Big Bill folded his newspaper and put it inside his briefcase.

"But I don't have one of *those*," Little Bill said, pointing to his dad's briefcase.

"Oh, yes you do," Alice the Great said, handing Little Bill his Captain Brainstorm lunch box.

Smooch!

Alice the Great gave Little Bill a big kiss. "Thanks," he said. "You're the best great-grandma ever."

He put his crayons and coloring book inside his pretend briefcase, right next to his sandwich.

Little Bill walked out the front door with his mom and dad.
"Bye, Mama. Bye, Alice the Great," Little Bill said, waving good-bye.

"Have a great day, you two," Brenda called after them.
"Don't you work Little Bill too hard now," Alice the Great shouted to Big Bill.
As they walked down the street, Big Bill greeted his neighbors. Little Bill waved to them. And the neighbors waved back.

They walked to the bus stop. Then Big Bill sat down on the bench, and Little Bill sat beside him.

"Guess what, Dad," Little Bill said, "you take a bus to work, and I take a bus to school. But my bus is yellow, and sometimes it takes us to the zoo."

Aboard the bus Little Bill asked, "Dad, what will I do at your office?"
"Well, I need a lot of help. There are pencils to sharpen and phone calls to answer."

They stepped off the bus, and Big Bill pointed to the tall gray building in front of them. "Well, here we are," he said.

Little Bill always liked the way his father's building seemed to touch the clouds. He pulled Big Bill's hand. "Come on, Dad. I'm ready to work!"

At his dad's office, Little Bill said hello to the receptionist, Ms. Gabrielle.

She smiled. "Hi, Little Bill. It's nice to see you."

"My dad needs my help today," Little Bill said proudly.

"I'm sure you'll do a fine job," said Ms. Gabrielle.

DEPARTMENT OF HOUSING

Little Bill and his dad walked by a room with a big glass window.

"Look, Dad. It's just like circle time in my class. Do you sing 'Good Morning to You?' Is that the teacher?"

"No, son," answered Big Bill. "That's the boss, Mrs. Miner. And they're having a meeting. But it's almost the same thing."

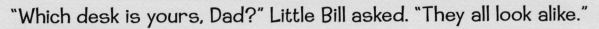

"Which desk is yours, Dad?" Little Bill asked. "They all look alike."

Big Bill grinned. "Here's a hint," he said. "On my desk you'll find something bright yellow, and it smells real good."

Little Bill popped his head into every cubicle. "It's not this one," he said over and over again.

Suddenly Little Bill stopped. "I found it! I found your desk!"
"Good work, son. How did you know?" Big Bill asked.
Little Bill pointed to the yellow flowers on the desk. "Because those are from
our yard . . . and that's us!" he added, pointing to a photograph.

While Big Bill was working, Little Bill was working too. He pulled his coloring book and crayons from his lunch box and put on his dad's headset.

"Hello, welcome to the Department of Housing," Little Bill said. He pretended to answer the phone and handed make-believe messages to his dad.

Then Little Bill followed his dad to the copy machine room.

"I could use your help making some copies," Big Bill said, pointing to the copy machine. "Want to start it up?"

Little Bill put his finger on the green button and counted, "Three-two-one . . . GO!"

The machine rattled loudly. And Little Bill started singing, "Click-clack, shoo-shoo, va-boom! Click-clack, shoo-shoo, va-boom!"

"That's the sound the copy machine makes," Little Bill said. He began to dance to the rattle of the copy machine—and Big Bill joined in!

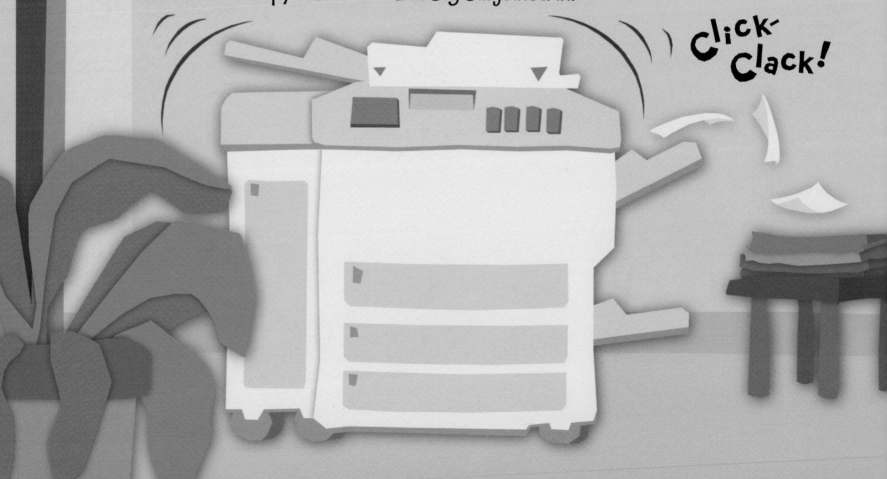

Click-Clack!

Shoo-Shoo Va-boom!

Soon everyone was peeking in to see Little Bill and his dad dancing and singing. Even Mrs. Miner looked in. "Well, I guess a little fun never hurt anybody," she said. Then she danced down the hallway.

"What do we do now, Dad?" asked Little Bill.

"It's lunchtime," Big Bill said with a wink.

As they sat on a bench eating their sandwiches, Little Bill
looked up at his dad. "You know what, Dad?"

"What, Little Bill?" Big Bill asked.

"You were right. Going to work *is* a lot like going to school.
And you even get to do the copy machine dance."

Little Bill was happy. He hugged his dad. "Next time you're coming to school with me!" he said.